THE
YOWIE
FINDS A HOME

THE YOWIE FINDS A HOME

Written by ANN FERNS

Illustrated by TRISTAN PARRY

It seemed to the Yowie that the whole world had turned grey. Wisps of damp grey mist were creeping up the mountainside, ghostly grey gum trees stretched their branches to a watery grey sky and over it all fell a cold grey drizzle of rain.

"Winter's coming!" cackled the Kookaburra from his perch on an old tree stump.

"What's so funny about *that*?" asked the Yowie as he huddled under a rock, trying to keep himself dry.

"You have to look on the bright side!" chortled Kookaburra.

The Yowie couldn't quite see the bright side of sitting in a puddle with cold water dripping down his back and the wind whistling through his whiskers. However, he decided that a little Yowie song might help, so in his cheeriest voice he began to sing:

"Ho! Let's all sing about rain and sleet,
And mud and slush that sticks to our feet.
When the winds are cold and the air is foggy,
The sky is grey and the ground is soggy,
When days are short and the nights are long,
Let's sing a Winter song!
Ho! Let's sing a song about snuffles and sneezes,
Influenza, coughs and wheezes,
A cold in the head, a sniffly nose,
Chilblains on all our fingers and toes.
We'll all have pneumonia before too long,
So let's sing a Winter song!"

"Hmm," said Kookaburra, as the last of the Yowie's song rumbled away down the valley. "Is that what you call looking on the bright side?"

"There isn't a bright side," answered the Yowie gloomily. "I'm cold and wet and I've nowhere to go."

"Then go home!" chuckled Kookaburra. "Home is the best place to be on a day like this."

"Home?" asked the Yowie. "Where's that?"

Kookaburra gave a squawk. "You don't know where your home is? Me oh my, you must be joking!" And he laughed so loudly that Wombat came shuffling out of the wet bushes to see what all the noise was about. The Yowie liked Wombat — he wasn't very clever, but he always tried to make up for it by being helpful.

"Hello," said Wombat. "Did someone make a joke?"

Kookaburra gave another whoop of laughter. "The Yowie says he doesn't know where his home is!"

Wombat's bright little eyes filled with sympathy. "That's not funny," he said. "That's very sad. But don't worry, Yowie, we'll soon find your home. What does it look like?"

"I've no idea," confessed the Yowie. "I've never seen it."

Kookaburra laughed so hard he almost fell over.

"It's *not* funny!" said Wombat again. "If poor Yowie doesn't have a home then we must find him one."

"That would be very nice." said the Yowie gratefully.

"Nothing to it!" said Kookaburra. "All you need is a hole in a tree trunk. Why there's one in that old gum tree over there!"

He fluttered over to the gum tree and poked his head into a large hole in its trunk. "Beautiful!" he boomed, his voice all deep and echoey from inside the hole. "Just the spot for a Yowie."

The Yowie crawled out from under the rock. He was very stiff and creaky from crouching for so long and he couldn't wait to be snug and warm in his very own nest in a tree trunk. But when he took a close look at the hole, his heart sank. "I'll never fit in there!" he cried.

"There you go again!" said Kookaburra. "Always looking on the dark side!"

Wombat was so eager to help that he forgot that he wasn't clever and actually had an idea.

"What we have to do," he said, "is fold him up like a piece of paper and *post* him through the hole!"

He was so excited by his very first idea that the Yowie didn't have the heart to tell him that it might not work.

Five minutes later when Mrs Wombat came to call her husband home to tea, a most astonishing sight met her eyes. Something Huge and Hairy was lying in the mud. Its feet had been pulled up over its shoulders and tucked behind its ears, its arms were neatly folded across the backs of its knees and Wombat was doing his best to push its head down towards its tummy button. Kookaburra sat on a branch overhead laughing hysterically.

"Wombat, dear," said Mrs Wombat "what *are* you doing?"

"I'm folding up the Yowie," explained Wombat. "Poor Yowie hasn't got a home — and if we can make him small enough, we're going to pop him into this hole."

"But perhaps the Yowie doesn't like being folded up," suggested Mrs Wombat gently. "Perhaps he'd rather live in a burrow, like we do."

The Yowie said in a wheezy, gurgly voice that he thought perhaps he would.

Wombat was disappointed that his idea hadn't worked. With a sigh he began to unfold the Yowie. Kookaburra just sat on his branch going "Ha! Ha! Tee! Hee!" which was rather irritating.

Mrs Wombat, who seemed to have taken charge of things, said that the Yowie would have to be measured for his burrow. So they straightened him out on the ground and Kookaburra drew a line round him with his beak. It was then that Mrs Wombat had *her* idea.

"I really think, Wombat dear," she said, "that instead of putting the Yowie under the ground, we should put the ground over the Yowie. It will be much quicker and easier."

Nobody asked the Yowie what he thought of that idea. But rather than hurt their feelings, he kept perfectly still while the Wombats got busy with their sharp front claws, shovelling wet earth on top of him.

It takes a long time to bury a Yowie. Kookaburra got thoroughly bored, with nothing very much to laugh at, and took himself off to bed. An hour later, when Possum just happened to be passing, there was still quite a lot of Yowie sticking out of the mound that the Wombats were furiously working on.

"Great galloping goannas!" yelled Possum. "Hold on mate, we'll soon have you out of there!" He took a flying leap onto the mound and began to scrabble away at the mud for all he was worth.

"But Possum dear," cried Mrs Wombat, "we're not trying to get the Yowie out. We're trying to put him in!"

"Great jumping jumbucks!" said Possum, when they told him the whole story. "You can't put a Yowie in a hole — and you can't bury him either. If you'd only asked me, I'd have told you straight off. The best place for a Yowie is in somebody's roof!"

"That may be all very well for a possum," said Mrs Wombat, "but People might not want a Yowie in their roof."

The Yowie had to agree — one really never knew with People.

"Great pink platypuses!" cried Possum. "My uncle lived in a roof all his life. The People treated him like one of the family. They even put a dish of milk and sugar out for him every night."

"Really?" said the Yowie, so interested that he sat up and ruined his burrow.

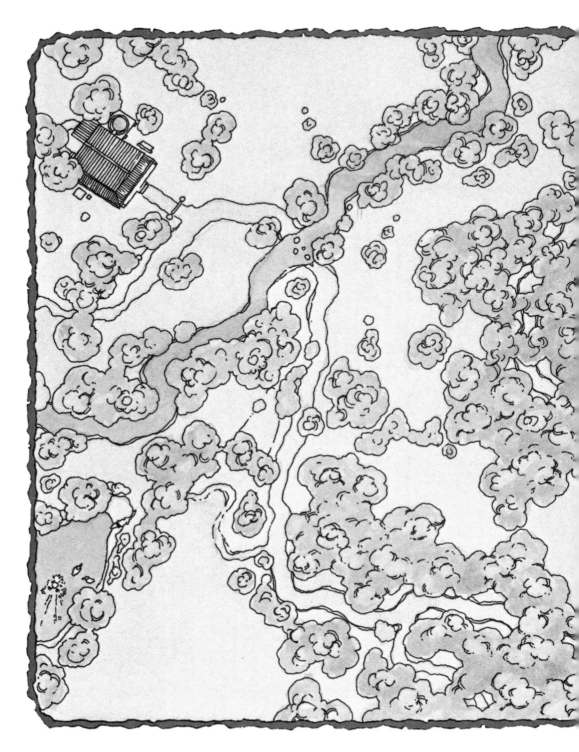

"I know just the place," said Possum. "A beaut little wooden house down in the valley. I'd thought of moving in there myself — but I don't mind if my old mate the Yowie takes it."

The Yowie was so overwhelmed by such generosity, he couldn't wait to see the house.

"Well, Yowie dear," said Mrs Wombat, "if you're sure you'll really be happy living in a roof, perhaps Possum should take you there right away. It *is* getting rather late." She and Wombat were secretly rather relieved that they didn't have to do any more digging.

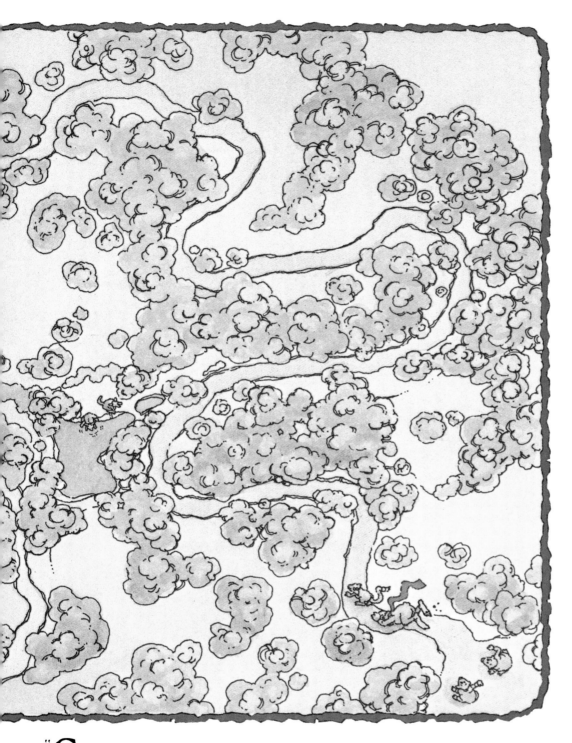

"See you in the spring!" called the Yowie happily as he set off down the
steep track, with Possum scampering ahead to show the way.

It was a long, winding climb down into the valley and several times the
Yowie stepped on his fingers and went tumbling head over heels. But he didn't
mind — it was good to be going home.

When at last they reached the little house nestling amongst some trees,
everything was in darkness.

"They've all gone to sleep," whispered Possum. "That's good, we'll just sneak
you up into the roof and nobody'll be any the wiser!"

Climbing into the roof was the easiest thing that had happened to the Yowie all day. He climbed up onto a garden bench which was standing against one of the end walls. Then all he had to do was reach up and gently push in the wooden board that sealed off the end of the roof.

"Good luck, old matey," whispered Possum, as the rear end of his friend disappeared through the opening.

It was too dark for the Yowie to see very much of his new home. It was,

perhaps, a little cramped, but it was warm and dry and smelt very cosily
of sawdust. "Ho Hum!" he yawned to himself. "Home sweet Home." He made
a little pillow from his hands, curled himself up and closed his eyes.

He was never quite certain what happened next. The floor beneath him
gave a sigh, then it gave a groan, then it just sort of . . . opened up!

The Yowie felt himself falling downwards, his arms and legs flapping in
all directions. "Yowee!" he cried.

He landed with a bump and a bounce on a large soft bed. There was a Lady in the bed and the Yowie was very happy that he hadn't *quite* landed on top of her. He wouldn't have wanted to upset the Lady or she might say that he couldn't live in her roof.

The Lady stared at him with eyes as large and round as the knobs on the bedhead. Then she opened her mouth very wide and made a very strange — and very unfriendly noise. "Aaaagh! Aaaagh! Aaaagh!"

It was all too much for the Yowie and he burst into tears. Sobbing bitterly, he scrambled off the bed. Large purple, blue and green opal tears fell plink and rattle all over the floor as he ran out of the house.

On and on he ran through the wild and windy bush. He didn't care where he went — he was so tired and so unhappy. The Lady would probably be furious at the dozens of opals he'd scattered all over her house — she'd never let him live in her roof now.

At last, just as it was getting light, he saw a clump of bushes growing close up against a tall, rocky cliff. It didn't look a very comfortable spot, but at least it would be out of the wind. On his hands and knees he crawled behind the bushes. To his surprise he found himself in the entrance to a tunnel, which seemed to lead right into the cliff. He could hardly believe his good fortune. A tunnel is not exactly cosy, but it is a place to sleep.

An even bigger surprise awaited him when he crawled into the tunnel, for very soon it opened out into a cave. It was a very large cave with high walls

of solid rock, a curved ceiling and a sandy floor. In one corner there was
a bed of dried leaves and grasses and in the other corner was a large tin
box.

Sitting on the lid of the box was a white Cockatoo, with a brilliant yellow
crest and small, bright, black eyes. "Hello! Hello!" said the Cockatoo, as though
the Yowie was the very person he'd been expecting. "Come in! Come in! Make
yourself at home!"

"Can I really?" asked the Yowie, his heart beating faster at the sound of
that magical word 'home'.

"Of course! Of course!" cried the Cockatoo. The Yowie wondered if he always said everything twice.

"Is this your cave?" he asked the Cockatoo shyly.

"Yes and no," said the Cockatoo. "It's really the Bushranger's cave, but he doesn't use it because he's been dead and gone these past eighty years." He fluffed up his feathers and added with pride, "I was the Bushranger's Cocky. I'll be one hundred and three next birthday! Oh, the tales I could tell you! The things I've seen! The places I've been!"

The Yowie would have loved to listen to a Cockatoo tale, but just at that moment he was so very, very tired. "Do you think . . ." he asked, trying his hardest not to yawn, "do you think I might just have a little sleep?"

"Sleep? Sleep?" screeched the Cockatoo. "Of course you can sleep!" He hopped down from the box and waddled towards the tunnel. "I'm off now anyway. Never stay long — too much to see, too much to do."

"But . . . but, will you be back?" stammered the Yowie.

"Perhaps. Perhaps not," answered the Cockatoo as he disappeared into the tunnel. "Don't wait up for me — I might be a year or two!"

With that he was gone and the Yowie was alone. Yet somehow he didn't feel alone. From somewhere in the shadows he heard a deep, warm voice saying to him, "Welcome home. Welcome home."

The Yowie smiled to himself. The ghost of the Bushranger was still in the cave. He could feel its friendliness even though he could not see it. How nice it would be to have company. He felt sure that a ghost and a Yowie could live very happily together.

He lifted the lid of the tin box and looked inside. Folded up on top was a large, thick patchwork rug. The Yowie lifted it out and underneath he found a mouth organ, a billy can and a large canvas bag. He knew that these things belonged to the Bushranger, just as the deep, warm voice belonged to him too.

"I'll look after them for you," promised the Yowie. Then he took off his slippers and and placed them in the box.

He wrapped himself up in the patchwork rug and lay down on the leafy, grassy bed. He was warm, he was dry, he was cosy. Faintly, from far, far away, he could hear the shrill wind whistling — but it couldn't get inside his cave.

He gave a huge sigh of contentment and closed his eyes. "Perhaps I'll make up a song," he thought drowsily. But the only words that drifted through his sleepy, happy head were the ones that the Bushranger seemed to be saying: "Welcome home. Welcome home."

Published in Australia in 2004 by
New Holland Publishers (Australia) Pty Ltd
Sydney • Auckland • London • Cape Town

14 Aquatic Drive Frenchs Forest NSW 2086 Australia
218 Lake Road Northcote Auckland New Zealand
86 Edgware Road London W2 2EA United Kingdom
80 McKenzie Street Cape Town 8001 South Africa

ISBN 1 74110 266 9

A CiP record of this title is available from the National Library of Australia

Reproduction by Sang Choy International, Singapore
Printed in Malaysia by Times Offset

2 4 6 8 10 9 7 5 3 1